THE GOLDEN LION TAMARIN COMES HOME

George Ancona

MACMILLAN PUBLISHING COMPANY • NEW YOR...

MAXWELL MACMILLAN CANADA • TORONTO

MAXWELL MACMILLAN INTERNATIONAL
NEW YORK • OXFORD • SINGAPORE • SYDNEY

The author gratefully acknowledges *The New Yorker* for permission to reprint on page 38 a quotation by Dr. Benjamin Beck, which appeared in the issue of June 24, 1991, in the article "A Reporter at Large: Golden Monkeys" by nature writer Diane Ackerman.

Macmillan Publishing Company is part of the Maxwell Communication Group of Companies.
Macmillan Publishing Company, 866 Third Avenue, New York, NY 10022.
Maxwell Macmillan Canada, Inc., 1200 Eglinton Avenue East, Suite 200, Don Mills, Ontario M3C 3N1.
First edition
Printed in Hong Kong by South China Printing Company (1988) Ltd.

10 9 8 7 6 5 4 3 2 1

The text of this book is set in 13 point Souvenir Light.

Library of Congress Cataloging-in-Publicaton Data
Ancona, George.
The golden lion tamarin comes home / George Ancona —
1st ed.   p.   cm.   ISBN 0-02-700905-X
1. Leontopithecus rosalia—Juvenile literature. 2. Wildlife reintroduction—Brazil—Juvenile literature. [1. Monkeys. 2. Wildlife reintroduction.] I. Title.
QL737.P92A53 1994 639.9'7982—dc20 93-23705
Summary: The story of the reintroduction into the wild of golden lion tamarins born in captivity.

This book became a reality through the help and cooperation of many people. To Dr. Benjamin Beck, associate director for biological programs and reintroduction coordinator of the Golden Lion Tamarin Conservation Program at the National Zoological Park, Smithsonian Institution, Washington, D.C., who opened the doors to the project and introduced me to Andreia Martins, coordinator of the program in Brazil. To Andreia Martins and her family, who graciously hosted me in Silva Jardim. To the observers who took me into the rain forest and, more importantly, brought me out: Arleia, Paulo Caesar, Paulo Edwardo, Elizamá, Nelson, Marão, Jabez, and Márcio. To Luis Fernando, who was kind enough to provide transportation. To the researchers who shared their work with me: Carlos Ruiz, Zique Moraes, and Adriana Daudt Gratival. To Denise Marcal Rambaldi, educational coordinator, and her staff, Patricia Martins, Valeria Cristina de Oliveira Pinto, and Ana Claudia Xavier Santos. To Dionizio Moraes Pessamilio, director of the reserve, for sharing his knowledge with me. To my wife, Helga, for the Portuguese translations. To all of you, *muito obrigado.* Thank you.

To Modesto Carvalhosa, my favorite mico

Whistling softly as she scans the upper canopy of leaves, Andreia Martins leads her sister Carolina and brother Renato through the rain forest. It is hot and humid. The small group is surrounded by the teeming life of the tropical forest.

Birds sing, insects buzz, cicadas chirp. Nearby they hear a tractor engine, cattle lowing, a rooster, and men at work on a *fazenda,* or "farm." They pick their way carefully along the narrow path to avoid the sharp spines of leaves and the tangle of vines underfoot.

Andreia raises her hand, and the group stops. Above them the leaves rustle and branches sway as streaks of orange-gold flash in the speckles of sunlight. "*Micos,*" she whispers to the children, and points to the cluster of golden lion tamarins staring down at them from the branches of the trees. Their high-pitched whistles and squeaks pierce the air.

"Mico" is short for *mico leão dourado,* the Portuguese name for the golden lion tamarin of Brazil. About the size of a squirrel, the monkey is named for its color and lionlike mane.

Washington, D.C.

Rio de Janeiro

■ Before Europeans arrived

■ Today

The golden lion tamarin is found only in the coastal rain forest of southeastern Brazil. Flanked by a mountain range on the west and the Atlantic Ocean on the east, the forest once stretched for 1,500 miles.

When the first Europeans arrived, they cut down the trees to build their homes and towns. They burned the rest of the forest to clear the land for settlements, for coffee and sugar plantations, and for pastures on which to graze livestock. The city of Rio de Janeiro grew and spread. Today only 2 percent of the original rain forest remains, scattered like small islands in a sea of farms and towns.

As its native habitat disappeared, so did the golden lion tamarin. By 1960 there were so few left that Dr. A. Coimbra-Filho, a Brazilian biologist, warned of its imminent extinction. He urged the Brazilian government to set aside the remaining forest as a wildlife refuge. The Poço das Antas Biological Reserve, a protected habitat, was established in 1973.

The tall trees in the tropical rain forest offer the tamarins food, protection from predators, and a network of routes through their territories. The cupped centers of bromeliads, plants that live in host trees, hold water and insects for the monkeys to drink and eat. Tamarins are omnivorous. They eat not only fruits, seeds, and nuts but also bird eggs, insects, frogs, and snakes, which provide additional protein.

The rain forest is alive both day and night with a diversity of wildlife. Among the trees can be seen sloths and other species of monkeys.

Tamarins must always be on guard for predators. Above them fly owls, while on the ground prowl ocelots, feral dogs, and—the most dangerous of all—humans. Poachers trap the tamarins and sell them in illegal animal markets for high prices. If discovered, these pets are confiscated and returned to the reserve.

Today golden lion tamarins are bred in many zoos around the world. These animals do not have the skills to survive in the wild on their own. A captive tamarin lives in a confined space, climbs sturdy poles that don't move, and is served its food in a bowl at regular hours by a familiar keeper. It has never leaped from a vine to a delicate tree branch that sways under its weight. It doesn't know how to forage for its food. It hasn't experienced weather changes—cold, rain, thunder, and lightning. It would be killed by predators or get lost and starve. It needs the help of humans and that of native-born tamarins to learn to survive independently in its original habitat.

Since 1983, Dr. Benjamin Beck and his staff at the National Zoological Park in Washington, D.C., have been trying to find ways to prepare captive-born tamarins for their return to the rain forest. Dr. Beck coordinates the reintroduction of the tamarins into their natural habitat for the Golden Lion Tamarin Conservation Program.

The tamarins being reintroduced often come from other zoos and are examined carefully when they arrive at the National Zoo. A different number is tattooed onto each animal's leg and entered into a studbook, a record of all the tamarins born in captivity.

As an experiment, tamarins are being permitted to live free in a wooded section of the zoo. Because they are territorial, they stay close to their nesting boxes, which are wired vertically high in the trees. The nesting box is a modified picnic cooler with two chambers inside, one above the other. In the top chamber is a hole through which the tamarins enter and leave. Should a predator attack, the tamarins huddle in the lower chamber, where a groping paw cannot reach them.

A tamarin claims its territory by rubbing a scent from its body onto tree limbs. The ones that will someday be reintroduced into the wild wear radio collars that transmit a constant beep, enabling the keepers to locate them in the woods. The tamarins are fed by food trays raised to the height of their nesting boxes.

Ropes are hung to simulate vines and to provide a network of treetop highways for the monkeys. The ropes and the nesting boxes are often changed while the tamarins are asleep to help prepare them for the unexpected.

The dilemma for the zoo is how to protect the animals and still expose them to the experiences and dangers they will meet in the wild.

Observers watch and record everything the monkeys do. To tell the tamarins apart, they mark the tails with hair dye. Each member of the tamarin family has its own distinctive tail marking.

When the time is right, the monkeys are shipped by air from Washington, D.C., to Rio de Janeiro.

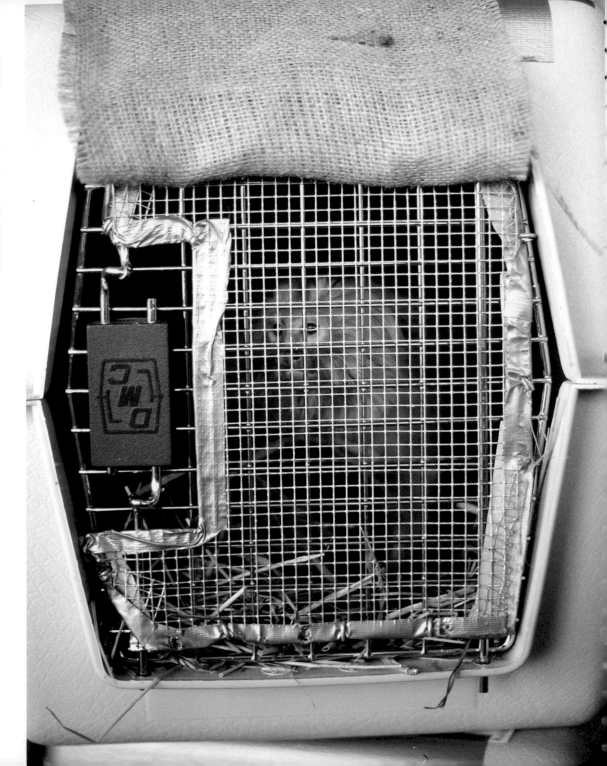

Andreia Martins is one of the many people in Brazil and abroad working to save the golden lion tamarin. She coordinates a team of observers who roam the rain forest, tracking tamarins and observing their behavior. The team's notes are sent to the National Zoo, where scientists in the conservation program use them to help prepare captive-born tamarins for their reintroduction into the rain forest.

In Rio de Janeiro, Andreia and Dionizio Moraes Pessamilio, director of the reserve, carry bags of fruit when they meet a shipment of seven tamarins that arrives from Washington, D.C.

After the overnight flight, the squealing monkeys are hungry, and they gobble up the pieces of fruit that Andreia and Dionizio squeeze into the cages. Then the noisy cages are loaded into a van for the two-hour trip to the reserve.

Golden lion tamarins tend to be monogamous, which means a male and female will live together and mate only with each other. This shipment includes a family of four from one zoo: the mother, the father, and a pair of one-year-old twins, one male and one female. The other three tamarins come from three different zoos and will be used to create new families.

Because there are so few tamarins left in the wild, they keep reproducing among themselves. Introducing animals that are born in distant zoos helps to strengthen the gene pool of the native tamarins. Genes carry the characteristics of a species from one generation to the next.

The van and the observation team meet on a narrow road in the forest. The tamarins are unloaded and carried into the woods, where large cages await the immigrants. They are released into the cages, where they will grow accustomed to their new surroundings.

Everything is different: the heat, the tall trees, the noises. The tamarins will get to know their potential prey, such as the insects and small reptiles and mammals that scoot in and out of their cages. Beyond the cages stalk their predators, which they must learn to avoid.

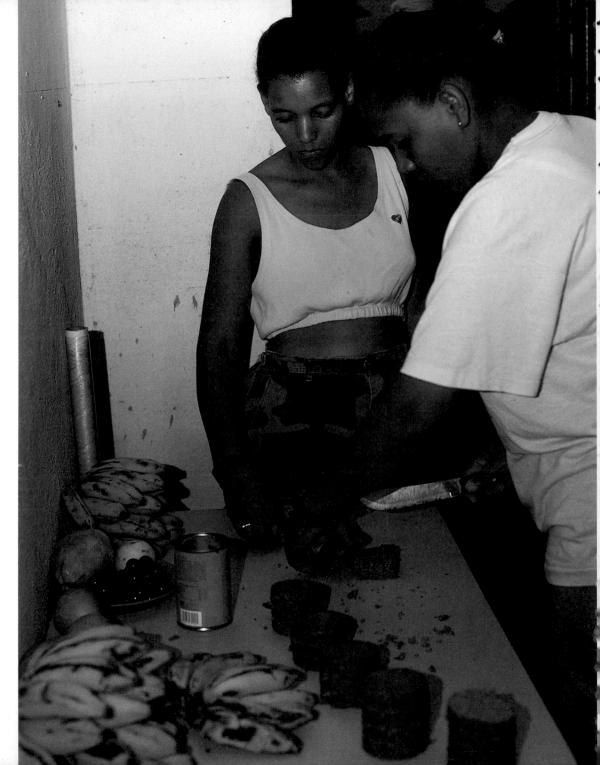

The reserve is located a few kilometers from the town of Silva Jardim, where Andreia lives with her mother and ten brothers and sisters. Every morning Andreia and her sister Arleia, who is also an observer, cut up fruit and canned marmoset food. The canned food, which provides needed protein, is exactly what the tamarins ate in the zoo.

The pieces of food are then stuffed into feeders made of plastic tubes wired together to make a square, with holes drilled along the tubes. Andreia crams bits of food into the holes. This encourages the tamarins to use their long fingers and nails to extract the food, just as they will probe in trees and rotted logs once they are released.

Meanwhile, Arleia fills canteens with water. By 7:30 A.M. the van is loaded with feeders and canteens. The sisters tuck their camouflage pants into their socks to keep out insects and jump into the van.

The Golden Lion Tamarin Conservation Program has provided many jobs for people in Silva Jardim. A small town, it is located near the main highway to Rio. The *praça,* or "plaza," with its tall shade trees, bandstand, and playground, sits in the center of town.

Andreia stops at the plaza to pick up more of the observation team. While waiting for them to arrive, she works out the assignment for each one. Every day, an observer is assigned to a different group of tamarins.

The observation team is split into two groups. One group goes to the reserve, while the other goes to the fazendas where tamarins have been reintroduced. Originally the *fazenderos,* or "farmers," were hesitant about accepting the monkeys on their forestland. But now they speak of them as "my micos."

Andreia drives through the forest, stopping every so often to drop off an observer. Each carries a canteen and a machete on a belt, as well as a backpack with food, raingear, a snakebite kit, and mosquito repellent. Everyone carries a compass, a digital watch, a notebook, and an antenna and radio receiver for tracking the tamarins. A full tamarin feeder, carried on the shoulder, completes the equipment each observer takes into the woods.

Today the newly arrived tamarin family of four will be released. They have spent enough time in the large cage to become accustomed to the climate of the rain forest. In addition to its own tail marking, each monkey has another mark on its body that identifies the family to which it belongs. One tamarin in the group wears a new radio collar.

Andreia and Paulo Caesar, another observer, carry the nesting box into the woods. They have selected a tree in an area that the tamarin family can claim as its own. Paulo Caesar nimbly climbs the tree with a rope and wire on his shoulder. When he reaches a fork about twenty feet above the ground, he drops one end of the rope to Andreia. She ties the end to the nesting box, and Paulo Caesar hoists it up and wires it in place. With the rope draped over a branch, he drops both ends to Andreia so she can raise a feeder up to the box. Finally, Paulo Caesar uncovers the opening of the nesting box and slides down to the ground. Then they both sit down to see what will happen.

A young tamarin pokes its head out of the box, looks around, and squeals. Then the other golden heads appear to take a look. After some tentative moves, the juvenile darts out to the feeder, pokes into it, and stuffs food into its mouth.

Below, Andreia glances at her watch and writes in her notebook. For the first hour, she describes what the entire group is doing—the way they eat, socialize, and rest, and the sounds they make. Then she notes what each member of the family does.

In order not to give the tamarins human characteristics, the observers do not give them names. Instead they identify the monkeys by letters that represent the zoo they came from and numbers that symbolize their position in the group. For example, KO1 is the adult female from the zoo in Cologne, Germany, KO2 is the adult male, and KO3 and KO4 are their offspring.

At first the newcomers stay close to their nesting box. Away from their new home, they may become disoriented and get lost. Alone, a newly reintroduced tamarin can die of starvation, become injured, or fall prey to a predator.

This is when the tamarins need the most help. They are given plenty of food and water. Oranges and bananas are hung on branches for them. Because the tamarins have always eaten chopped fruit, they don't know how to peel whole fruit. The bananas are partially opened for them, and the oranges have "windows" cut into them.

As the months go by, the feeder is placed farther from the nesting box. Fruits are placed on saplings that will sway when the tamarins leap onto them.

When the tamarins begin to forage and eat natural foods, the observers reduce their visits to three times a week, then to once a week, and finally to once a month. When the tamarins become independent, all feeding is stopped.

Bit by bit, the family becomes familiar with the rain forest, the younger ones adapting faster than the parents. But only about 30 percent of all reintroduced tamarins survive more than two years. Some die by eating poisonous fruits or snakes. Some are killed by Africanized, or "killer," bees, which sometimes take over a nesting box to make a hive. The infants that are born in the wild fare much better than the reintroduced tamarins. They are more acrobatic and confident as they leap from limb to limb. They are able to deal with surprises, and they don't have to unlearn behaviors that were adequate for zoo life but are useless in the forest.

Each group of tamarins is a family. Usually twins, and sometimes triplets, are born once a year. Because the mother cannot carry all the babies, the father and older children help. At eighteen to twenty-four months, the children reach puberty. The mother chases the mature daughters away from the group to find mates elsewhere and form families of their own. The sons stay on a little longer to help carry the babies, but soon they, too, must leave.

Tamarins move through the rain forest as a group, the infants always carried by the older ones. When they stop, they nestle close together to rest, sleep, groom one another, and keep warm. They take turns probing and looking through one another's fur for ticks and fly eggs, which they eat. Tamarins that are captured and sold as pets often die because they are separated from their families.

The leaders of the group, the father and mother, vocalize the loudest when other tamarins get too close to the family's territory. While the adults scream and threaten out-siders, the young from the different groups play together. This prepares them for the time when they will choose mates and form new groups.

Scientists from all over the world come to the reserve to study life in the rain forest. Their presence helps to discourage hunters and poachers. So that they can learn how tamarins communicate vocally in the wild, one team of scientists records the voices of tamarins on the reserve.

The goals of the conservation program are to have two thousand tamarins in the rain forest and to quadruple the area of the rain forest by the year 2025. Large tracts of land will have to be reforested by spreading lime and planting trees. The reforested areas will form land bridges to close the gaps between the existing islands of forest. This will enable tamarins that are isolated to contact one another.

The future of the golden lion tamarin depends partly on the awareness of the local farmers and townspeople of its plight. An educational group on the reserve visits the fazenderos to ask them to accept the tamarins and not cut down their woodlands. The group visits schools to show children slides of the plants and animals in the forest. It also puts on a play that dramatizes the story of the tamarin with costumes, words, and songs. The play tells the story of a little boy named Marcelo who goes into the rain forest and meets a tamarin and another type of monkey, a butterfly, a frog, and a sloth. The animals teach Marcelo about life in the forest.

A small museum on the reserve shows visitors the biodiversity of the rain forest. Not only do schoolchildren visit it, but townspeople and travelers stop by to learn about the forests they pass on the highway.

The object of all the work being done today is a future in which human beings can live surrounded by a rich diversity of wildlife. As Dr. Benjamin Beck says, "Conservation is really a timeless concept. You're conserving forever. You're conserving so that evolution can proceed naturally. I personally will never know whether the Golden Lion Tamarin Conservation Program was successful. All I can look at is short-term goals. One goal is reintroduced tamarins that are totally self-sufficient. We have several such groups now, and I would say they are wild."

But youngsters like Carolina and Renato will know when they grow up. They will know that the efforts of Andreia and Arleia and many other people have left them a rich legacy, a world all the better because of the trees, birds, animals, and especially the golden lion tamarins that live next door.

ZOOS IN THE UNITED STATES WHERE GOLDEN LION TAMARINS CAN BE SEEN

Acadia Zoological Park
Trenton, Maine

Audubon Park & Zoological Garden
New Orleans, Louisiana

Baltimore Zoo
Baltimore, Maryland

Beardsley Zoological Gardens
Bridgeport, Connecticut

Bergen County Zoological Park
Paramus, New Jersey

Brandywine Zoo
Wilmington, Delaware

Burnet Park Zoo
Syracuse, New York

Cheyenne Mountain Zoological Park
Colorado Springs, Colorado

Chicago Zoological Park
Brookfield, Illinois

Cincinnati Zoo & Botanical Garden
Cincinnati, Ohio

Columbus Zoological Gardens
Powell, Ohio

Denver Zoological Gardens
Denver, Colorado

Dickerson Park Zoo
Springfield, Missouri

Discovery Island
Lake Buena Vista, Florida

Dreher Park Zoo
West Palm Beach, Florida

El Paso Zoological Park
El Paso, Texas

Folsom Children's Zoo & Botanical
Gardens
Lincoln, Nebraska

Fort Worth Zoological Park
Fort Worth, Texas

Glen Oak Zoo
Peoria, Illinois

Greater Baton Rouge Zoo
Baker, Louisiana

Great Plains Zoo & Museum
Sioux Falls, South Dakota

Greenville Zoo
Greenville, South Carolina

Henry Doorly Zoo
Omaha, Nebraska

Henson Robinson Zoo
Springfield, Illinois

Hogle Zoological Gardens
Salt Lake City, Utah

Honolulu Zoo
Honolulu, Hawaii

Houston Zoological Gardens
Houston, Texas

International Wildlife Park
Bronx, New York

Los Angeles Zoo
Los Angeles, California

Louisiana Purchase Gardens & Zoo
Monroe, Louisiana

Louisville Zoological Garden
Louisville, Kentucky

Lowry Park Zoological Garden
Tampa, Florida

Memphis Zoological Garden &
Aquarium
Memphis, Tennessee

Miami Metrozoo
Miami, Florida

Micke Grove Zoo
Lodi, California

Mill Mountain Zoo
Roanoke, Virginia

Milwaukee County Zoological Gardens
Milwaukee, Wisconsin

Monkey Jungle
Miami, Florida

National Aquarium in Baltimore
Baltimore, Maryland

National Zoological Park
Washington, D.C.

New England Science Center
Worcester, Massachusetts

Oklahoma City Zoological Park
Oklahoma City, Oklahoma

Philadelphia Zoological Garden
Philadelphia, Pennsylvania

Phoenix Zoo
Phoenix, Arizona

Pittsburgh Zoo
Pittsburgh, Pennsylvania

Point Defiance Zoo & Aquarium
Tacoma, Washington

Potawatomi Zoo
South Bend, Indiana

Potter Park Zoo
Lansing, Michigan

Pueblo Zoo
Pueblo, Colorado

Racine Zoological Garden
Racine, Wisconsin

Rare Species Conservatory
Loxahatchee, Florida

Riverbanks Zoological Park
Columbia, South Carolina

Roger Williams Park Zoo
Providence, Rhode Island

Ross Park Zoo
Binghamton, New York

Saint Louis Zoological Park
Saint Louis, Missouri

San Antonio Zoological Gardens &
Aquarium
San Antonio, Texas

San Diego Wild Animal Park
Escondido, California

Santa Ana Zoo
Santa Ana, California

Santa Barbara Zoological Gardens
Santa Barbara, California

Scovill Children's Zoo
Decatur, Illinois

Sedgwick County Zoo
Wichita, Kansas

Trevor Zoo
Millbrook, New York

Tulsa Zoological Park
Tulsa, Oklahoma

University of Nebraska at Omaha
Omaha, Nebraska

Utica Zoo
Utica, New York

Wild Animal Habitat
Kings Island, Ohio

Wildlife Safari
Winston, Oregon

Wildlife World Zoo
Litchfield Park, Arizona

Woodland Park Zoological Gardens
Seattle, Washington

The ZOO
Gulf Breeze, Florida

Zoo Atlanta
Atlanta, Georgia

ZooWorld
Panama City Beach, Florida